I enjoy sharing my books as I do my friends, asking only that you treat them well and see them safely home

the Star of this Book

THE GREAT SESAME STREET ABC HUNT

Mr. Hooper, it's time for the Great Sesame Street ABC Hunt! Are you going to play?

I'm afraid I'm too busy to play, Big Bird. But I'll supply the prize. If you win, I'll give you a special ice cream sundae -- named after you!

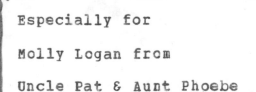

Especially for
Molly Logan from
Uncle Pat & Aunt Phoebe

BY NORMAN STILES AND DANIEL WILCOX

PICTURES BY CAROL NICKLAUS